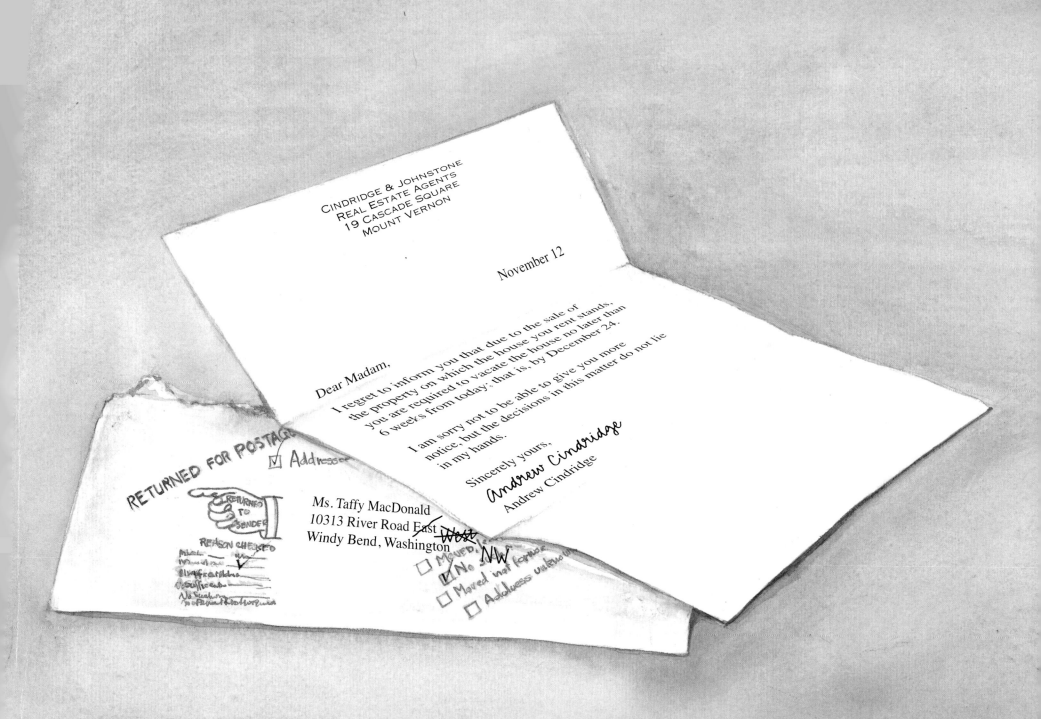

CINDRIDGE & JOHNSTONE
REAL ESTATE AGENTS
19 CASCADE SQUARE
MOUNT VERNON

November 12

Dear Madam,

I regret to inform you that due to the sale of the property on which the house you rent stands, you are required to vacate the house no later than 6 weeks from today; that is, by December 24.

I am sorry not to be able to give you more notice, but the decisions in this matter do not lie in my hands.

Sincerely yours,

Andrew Cindridge

Andrew Cindridge

RETURNED FOR POSTAGE

☑ Addressee

RETURNED TO SENDER

REASON CHECKED

Ms. Taffy MacDonald
10313 River Road East ~~West~~
Windy Bend, Washington NW

☐ Moved,
☑ No.
☐ Moved not known
☐ Address unknown

TAHNEE

NOTHING

TAFFY
(AND HER FAMILY)

OTTO

TORY

MAYBE

PERI

BUNNY

WUZZY

DIGGEDY

BUMP

THUMP

TAPS

MINKY-WEEZLE

JEEP

The Christmas
We Moved to the Barn

STORY BY
ALEXANDRA DAY AND COOPER EDENS

PICTURES BY
ALEXANDRA DAY

MICHAEL DI CAPUA BOOKS · HARPER COLLINS PUBLISHERS

FOR MY MOTHER · A.D.
FOR GRANDMA GARNET AND GRANDPA OTTO · C.E.

"You musn't worry about this.
I've got a plan, and I know we can do it."